a minedition book

published by Penguin Young Readers Group

Text copyright © 2008 for individual stories by the authors,
for the concept and connecting story by Brigitte Weninger
Illustrations copyright © 2008 by Eve Tharlet and J.P. Corderoch
copyright © 2006 „Zottelbär" by Waltraud Egitz published by Bohem Press, Switzerland
Original title: Engel, Bär und Kugelmond, 28 Gute-Nacht Geschichten
English text translation by Kathryn Bishop
Coproduction with Michael Neugebauer Publishing Ltd., Hong Kong.
Rights arranged with "minedition" Rights and Licensing AG, Zurich, Switzerland.

Published simultaneously in Canada.
Manufactured in China by Wide World Ltd.
Typesetting in Optima by Hermann Zapf
Color separation by Fotoreproduzioni Grafiche, Verona, Italy.

Library of Congress Cataloging-in-Publication Data available upon request.

ISBN 978-0-698-40081-8
10 9 8 7 6 5 4 3 2 1
First Impression

For more information please visit our website: www.minedition.com

28 Good Night Stories

Written and Compiled by Brigitte Weninger
Illustrations by Eve Tharlet
Translated by Kathryn Bishop

mine**dition**

An old bear sat in the meadow and looked up at the moon that hung so round and yellow in the sky.
"Oh, if I could just reach it, it looks like a yummy piece of honey-comb. I would certainly have a wonderful treat!" thought the old bear.
Suddenly he saw something bright shooting across the night sky. It got bigger and bigger and was coming straight towards him. Oh, help, what was it?

KABING – KABANG – KABOOM

"Oh, thunder claps and lightning bolts!" a little voice swore. "Always these stupid landings. Something always goes wrong!

The old bear blinked. He was certainly curious. In the meadow now stood a little angel wearing a red cap with a little star dangling from the top. "Ow-zi-bough!" she said.
"Ow-zi-bough? What does that mean?" the bear wanted to know. The angel paced about and said, "Who are you?"
"I'm Bear," said the old bear and bowed politely.
"And what brings you here?"
"Guess," said the little angel pointing at his red cap. The little star on top was shining.
"Hmmm, are you the Sky Sheriff?" wondered the bear.
"Maybe you're an official star-polisher, the one whomakes the stars twinkle?"
"No, even better," said the little angel.
"I'm a guardian angel. I wanted to be one for such a long time."
"What a wonderful job," said the bear.
"It must be difficult to be a good guardian angel.
"Well," said the little angel a bit embarrassed, "at the moment I am just a guardian angel-trainee. To pass the test I have to practice flying,

9

landing, and of course, Angel-eze, the angel
language.I also must watch over a child,
every night until the next full moon. And every night
I mustwhisper to the child the special word."
"You mean every night you must whisper the same word?"
asked the bear. The angel nodded.
"That must be boring," said the bear.
"It is, kind of, but the special word is so important, the child
must never forget it, and what else should I say?"
"Well," said the bear, "couldn't you tell the child stories, like
bedtime stories, silly stories, and any-whatcha-ma-call-it-kind
of stories..."
"That's a great idea," said the angel, "and I can still whisper the
special word to the child. Why don't you tell me a story so I can
tell it to the child? Please."

"Okay," said the bear, "but then after that you must tell me
one. I like stories better than, than..."
"Than sunbeam spaghetti?" the angel guessed.
"No, better than...honeycomb!"
"It's a deal!" said the little angel.

"We'll start tomorrow evening. I need to
go now to the child and whisper
to him. I'm so excited! See you
soon!"
And he was off. The old bear watched
him disappear and shook his head.

Evening 1
The Full Moon

On this evening the little angel fell like a sack of potatoes out of the sky. The old bear helped him up.

"Oh pfooey," said the angel. "Whatever am I doing wrong?"

"Perhaps you are too fast," said the bear. "I think the birds slow down a bit before they land."

"I'll give it a try tomorrow," said the angel, "But now I want to have my story and I want it to be a... cloud story. After that I must hurry and visit the child."

"Hmm, a cloud story," said the bear. "Yes, I think I can handle that." And so the old bear started the first story.

Cloud Children

by Bruno Hächler

One bright and sunny summer day, Lynn and her brother Matthew were on their way to play. They jumped, and hopped and laughed. Basil, their shaggy dog, was running and twisting between their legs.

"Look at my somersault," shouted Lynn as she rolled in the grass.
"You make a somersault like a potato," teased her brother.
"I'll get you," she hollered, chasing after him.
Out of breath, the two laid down in the meadow looking up at the clouds floating by.
"The cloud over there looks like a crocodile," said Matthew.
It was true, the big mouth, the sharp teeth and the tail were easy to see.
Lynn was surprised; the clouds were full of figures:

A flea, a mouse, a snail in a house
A dragon too, and was that a gnu?
Oh look, there's an elephant to see
And a dromedary, can that be?

Lynn and Matthew lay next to each other for a long time. They were tired and their eyes were heavy. Asleep, their dreams carried them up to the clouds where they floated around and around with all the cloud animals.

Tiger paws and kitty cat claws
Pigs and bats in funny hats
So many creatures, so much to see
and is that a kangaroo in the tree?

Then a big wind chased new clouds toward them, but they weren't afraid, because the clouds were only:

Trolls and ghosts and ugly witches
Monster heads with nasty stitches

13

Tongue of snake, and eye of gnat
Wild and spooky stuff like that

They both shuddered and then laughed. It wasn't that spooky!
Raindrops suddenly sprinkled down on their nose and cheeks mouth and
chin. They wiggled and giggled but it tickled so much they couldn't stand
it a moment longer. They opened their eyes and saw a friendly, shaggy
face with a long wet tongue.

"Oh, Basil," they laughed and hugged their dog.
"Tomorrow...tomorrow we'll visit the clouds again and you're
coming with us!"

15

"Last evening I told the child the cloud story," said the little angel, scraping
dirt off his pants. "And then I whispered the special word, but staying awake
so long is not so easy, falling asleep, now that's easy!"
"Not for me," said the old bear. "And when so much as a flea burps,
I wake up again!"

"Then I know just the right story for you,"
said the little angel.
"You mean a burping story?" asked the old bear,
very surprised. "No," said the little angel.
"Don't be silly! I know the magic formula for
falling asleep!"
And the little angel told the second story…

Blink Once, Blink Twice...

by Hubert Flattinger

Blink once, blink twice,
and close your eyes,
Good night!

These are the magic words to a wonderful land! A red curtain hides the entrance. Wait, the curtain is going up!

Look, you are standing on the beach, and the sea is making peaceful sounds. The seagulls circle in the sky. And over there is a little pail and shovel so you can play in the sand. Build a big castle. Can you hear the trumpets announcing the arrival of the noble knights? And up in the tower a princess is waving. Now the drawbridge opens and the knights ride out. They are in search of adventure.

Somewhere far ahead their tracks are lost in the sand...

Blink once, blink twice,
and close your eyes,
The sea might also be a meadow!

Do you see butterflies dancing in the breeze and it looks like the bugs are wearing colorful clothes to climb the tall grass?

The bees buzz between the flowers!

To see everything better, make yourself really small... Suddenly the world is very big. And now even bigger!

And in this wonderful land there is more than just a sea and a meadow.

Look, there are little rainbows over glasses full of raspberry juice.

In this wonderful land the sunshine laughs on cloudy days and there are no locks on the doors.

In the wonderful land you can have adventures and must never be afraid. You could play with a wild dragon and challenge him to a fire breathing contest. In the wonderful land it's normal.

17

Blink once, blink twice, and close your eyes,
…Now wings will carry you above the wonderful land.
From high above, the world looks quite different.
Giants are suddenly little dwarfs. Perhaps you'd like to ride on big bear
through the wonderful land?
There might be snow and then suddenly flowers will bloom everywhere.
In the light of day the moon laughs and tonight the sun will wear pajamas.

Blink once, blink twice,
and then perhaps… a yawn?
The wonderful land is still far away.
It is the place for a thousand sweet dreams.
Imagine something!
It's so simple.

Blink once, blink twice,
close your eyes,
and good night!
These are the magic words for a trip to
a wonderful land.

18

Evening 3

On this evening the little angel flew as elegantly as a hippo through the evening sky. CRASH-BOOM! He landed right on top of a mole hill.

"Don't say anything, not one word!" mumbled the little angel as the bear helped him up.

"Not one word," repeated the angel.

"Nothing at all, not even a story," teased the old bear. "What will you tell the child?"

"Okay, a story," sighed the angel, "but there must be a mole in the story."

"Good, a mole story," nodded the bear. "And you can tell me about your assignment."

"Okay," promised the angel, "but you start!"

And so the old bear began the third story.

20

Marco and the Book in the Woods *by Karl Ruehmann*

Marco, a little wild pig, was bored. "I think I'll go and visit my friend Frog!" he said. He set out right away for the pond and started calling,
"Helloooo... Frog! Do you want to play?"
But the frog was lying at the edge of the pond, starring at a piece of paper.
"Don't bother me, please!" he said. "I found a picture with words written under it. It's something about a ship."
Frog was so busy with his picture that Marco walked on to the tree where his friend Magpie always slept.
"Magpie," he called. "Come down and play!"
"I'm busy!" she cawed. "I found a picture of a bird with beautiful colors called a parrot," and Magpie kept reading.
Marco was getting angry. "Then I'll just go and play with the little fox," he said.
The little fox was sitting in front of his den with the same sort of colorful piece of paper.
"Hey, do you want to play?" asked Marco.
But the little fox said, "Shhh, I'm reading about an island with a treasure!"
Marco was mad and stomped away grumbling, "How silly! Nobody has time and I want to play!" He stomped his foot again, even harder. A mole stuck its head out and said, "Hey, what's going on up here? Who's making all the commotion?"
"Why?" Marco asked. "Are you reading too?"
"Yes," the mole said, "just imagine, I found a piece of paper with a picture on it. It's a picture of a man with an eye patch. There are words under the picture too."
The mole disappeared again.
Marco had finally had enough. "Then go ahead and read your dumb paper." he said.
"I'll go play by myself at the red bench!" When Marco got to the red bench,

there was something on it. It was an open book! Marco thought the cover
looked beautiful. But when he flipped through the pages… he noticed that
some of the pages were missing. The wind must have torn them out and
blown them away… Suddenly Marco's friends all came running.

"We want to play now," said Frog. "My paper is boring. I don't even know
how the story of the ship ends."

"I'd like to know what happened to the parrot," said Magpie.

"I don't know whether the island really has hidden treasure or if the man with
the eye patch is dangerous!" said the little fox.

Marco had an idea: "Go and get your pages and I will show you something."
Soon all the pages were spread out on the bench. Marco looked at each
picture and then read the words carefully. Then he put each of the pages in
22 the right place between the book covers he had found.

When he had finished Marco sat down on the red bench and
began to read the story. His friends listened to every word.

When Marco closed the book again, Magpie said, "That was the best story
I've ever heard!"

"I liked the pictures too!" said Frog.

"I think the way Marco read the story was great," Mole added.

The little fox just sighed, "It's a pity the story is over."

"What should we do now?"

"Well, why don't we play Treasure Island together!" said Marco happily.

"May I be the Pirate captain?"

23

"Do all humans have guardian angels?" asked the old bear on the fourth
evening.

"Of course," said the little angel.

"And the animals?"

"Certainly, every living thing has an angel beside it, one that watches over
them by day and whispers the special word at night."

"The special word," whispered the old bear. "It sounds so mysterious.
Can you tell me what it is?"

"I don't know whether I am
allowed to," said the little angel.

"I do know a great pirate story
I can tell you.
Want to hear it?"
And so the little angel
told the fourth story.....

The Red Pirate *by Heinz Janisch*

The little hippopotamus came out of the water and pushed the diver's mask up on his forehead. He heard a humming and then a roar in the sky. An old, rickety airplane flew over head. And sitting in the pilot's seat was someone wearing a bright red helmet.

"The red pirate!" shouted the little hippo.
"Stop, be still," his mother said, "I'm trying to dry you off."
Suddenly the little hippo was wrapped up to his ears in bath towel.

"The red pirate," said the little hippo from under the bath towel. But when the little hippo was finally dry, the airplane had disappeared.

"You heard the red pirate didn't you?" he asked. His father just yawned and said, "You read too many comics, my boy. I only hear the sound of the sea." That evening the little hippo looked through his comic books. He had collected all the adventure comics about the red pirate: The Red Pirate in the Desert, The Red Pirate in the Jungle, The Red Pirate in the Snow and many more. The little hippo compared the pictures. There was no question, he had seen the red pirate, the most courageous adventurer of all times!

Two days later, in school, the children all had to write an essay: What I would like to be when I grow up. The little hippo stared, deep in thought. The red pirate appeared flying his rickety old airplane over a clearing. He waved and the little hippo waved back.
"You're not writing," his teacher said. "Don't you know what you would like to be?"

"I want to be a red pirate," said the little hippo.
From that point on he had one goal: He had to ride, fence, dive, run, build fires and climb trees as well as the red pirate. The little hippo practiced and practiced.

One day as his family was sitting down for breakfast, a rickety airplane landed on the beach. An old pirate with a red helmet stepped out. Everyone was so surprised they just sat there as still as could be. Only the little hippo jumped up.

"I'm sorry to interrupt your breakfast," the pirate said, "but I need the help of the little hippo. I am already tired and there is so much to do."

"Aye, Sir!" said the little hippo. "I'm ready."
"I know," said the red pirate. "I saw you practicing."
"See you soon," the little hippo called back to his family.

The two red pirates were off and disappeared between the clouds.
"Well, I never," said his father. "Did you see that?" The others just nodded.
"My brother is a red pirate!" said the youngest hippo proudly.

Around noon the little hippo returned. He took off his red helmet and said, "Well, that's settled."
And then he said to his surprised parents, "Greetings from the red pirate. He apologizes again for interrupting breakfast."

"That's alright," said his mother. "After all, it was important..."

"It certainly was and he said that we are an unbeatable team."
Then the little hippo went to bed and slept straight through till supper.

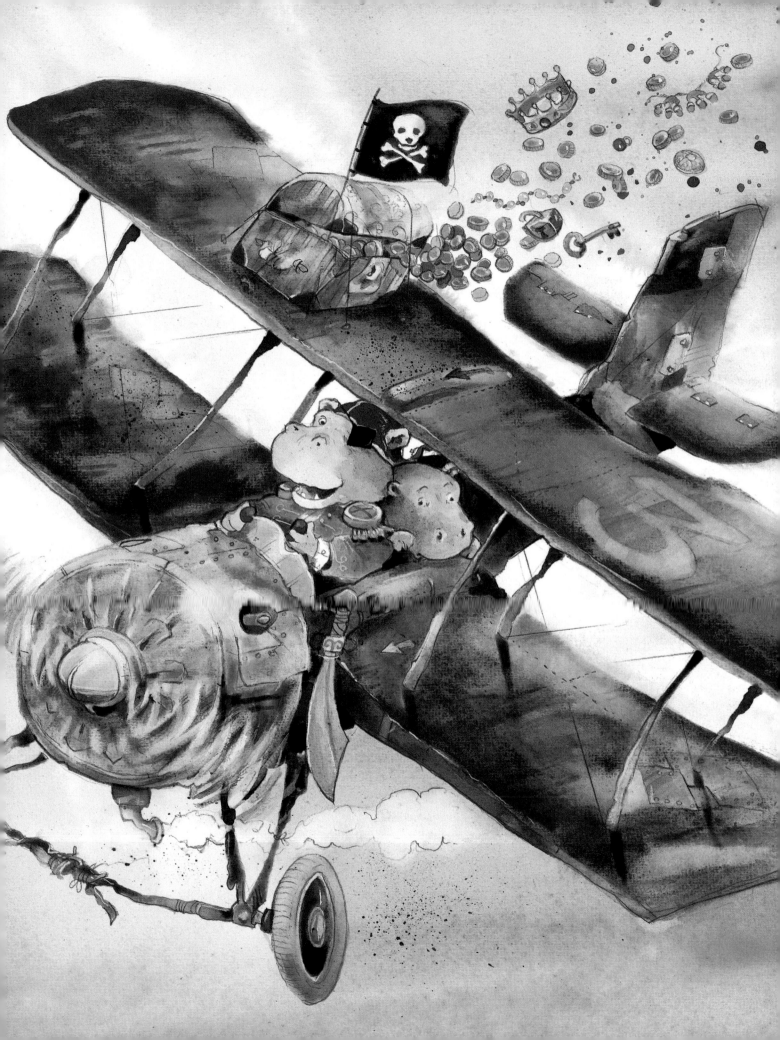

EVENING 5

It was a waning moon, which meant the moon was getting smaller. That evening the little angel was very still.

"Oh, Bear," he asked, sounding rather depressed. "Do you think I'll ever be able to learn how to fly and land correctly?"

"Sure you will," said the old bear, trying to calm his little friend. "You still have a lot of time to practice before the next full moon. How are you and the child doing?"

"Very well, thank you," reported the little angel. "Fortunately it is still small and doesn't wiggle too much. But yesterday he didn't want to go to sleep. His parents were already getting, you know, kind of piffzi puffzi."

"Hmm, I know a story about such a child," said the bear. And so the old bear began the fifth story.

28

Papa Has an Idea! *by Bernhard Costa*

"Johnny! It's time for bed."

"No, not tonight!" Johnny said as he started running. His father ran right after
him. "Oh yes, tonight too!"

Uh-oh! Shouting! "No, no!"

Papa had an idea, "A sack of flour! You're a sack of flour!" He picked Johnny
up. "Ha ha," he said as he ran through the living room and into the bathroom.
"I've got a sack of flour!" Then Papa ran into the kitchen and said, "WUUMPF!"
as Johnny landed on the bed. There was no more shouting.

"Book, book!" said Johnny. Papa had almost forgotten. So they looked at a book,
read it out loud, and Papa asked, "Would you like a little kiss too?"

"Yes," said Johnny, "Good night!"

The next evening was the same. Shouting and more shouting! "We go to bed
every night!" Papa said, but Johnny cried, "No!" Papa had an idea.

"Come, Johnny," he said, "come play 'Bear' with me in the big bed!" They both
played wildly around the bed. They sniffed and growled and tumbled about.
Then Johnny said, "A sack of flour!"

"Aha!" said Papa, picking Johnny up. "A sack of flour!" Bath, kitchen, living
room, "A sack of flour!" and WUUMPF, and Johnny landed in the little bed.
Looked at a book, read it out loud, a big hug and...

"A kiss too?" asked Papa

"Yes, good night!"

The next night Johnny was already in pajamas. "Play bear!"

"Tonight too?" Johnny nodded. Off to the big bed, they sniffed and growled and
tumbled about. Then Johnny said "A sack of flour!"

"Aha!" said Papa, picking Johnny up. "A sack of flour!" Bath, kitchen, living
room. "A sack of flour!" and WUUMPF, and Johnny landed in the little bed.
Looked at a book, read it out loud, a big hug and...

"A kiss too?" asked Papa

"Yes, good night!"

And the night after that?

29

"Time for pajamas!" said Papa.

"No, not tonight no, no, no!" Shouting, shouting, shouting!

Papa suddenly had a new idea. "Johnny's a piece of clay," he said,
"Knead, knead, knead and... tickle!"

Johnny laughed and giggled, "Enough!"

"A sack of flour, play bear, tumble and look at
books," said Johnny.

"That's quite a lot!" said Papa, picking Johnny up.

"A sack of flour!" Bath, kitchen, living room.

"A sack of flour!"

Now WUUMPF, and Johnny landed in
the little bed.

Looked at a book, read it out loud,
a big hug and...

"A kiss too?" asked Papa.

"Knead and tickle again!" said Johnny.

Papa looked surprised.

"Knead and tickle again," said Johnny.

"Now it's enough," said Papa quite loudly.

He sat on the little bed, and said,
"Papa's tired!"

"Papa go to bed"

"Johnny go to bed!"

Johnny patted Papa on the nose.

"Papa still has to work."

Johnny patted Papa on the head.

Papa whispered, "I'm going to the kitchen."

Johnny patted Papa again.

"Door open, please," said Johnny.

"Of course," said Papa, "and a little kiss?"

"Yes, please"

"A big kiss?"

30 "Yes, please... Good night!"

Evening 6

The next evening the little angel said, "Have you noticed that we always seem to have something similar to tell?"
The old bear agreed.
"You told a good night story, and then I told a good night story. You told the story about the pirate book, and then I told about the hippo pirate."
"Why, that's true," said the bear. "Stories seem to happen that way. First one says something, and then the other knows something too!"
"Then it doesn't matter that I also have a father and child story?" asked the little angel.
"Of course not," said the bear.
And so the little angel began to tell the sixth story.

32

If There Was No You...

by Karl Rühmann

"Good morning! Guess who's here?" said the boy behind the kitchen chair. His father yawned and rubbed his eyes. "Hmm, could it be that awful robber?"
"No!"
"Maybe the little red hen," said Dad.
"No!" said the boy, laughing. "It's me!" And he jumped out from hiding place.

"Well isn't this a surprise," said Dad and gave him a hug. "How nice!"

"What would you do if there wasn't a me?" asked the boy.
"Hmm." said Dad, thinking. "If there wasn't a you, I'd have to have breakfast with the...flowerpot. I would pour a bit of tea water in his saucer."

"But the flower pot couldn't tell you, what he dreamed," said the boy. His father nodded. "That's true. And later I would have to go shopping, all by myself. Perhaps I could ask the vacuum cleaner if she would like to come along."

"But you couldn't buy the vacuum cleaner an ice cream cone," said the boy. "And you like that so much."

"You're right," Dad said. "And later I would have to play games with the toaster."

"He wouldn't laugh if you always won," said the boy, "and that's half the fun."

"I agree," said Dad. "And later I'd have to ask someone else to watch television with me, perhaps... the broom."

"But brooms have only straw in their heads," said the boy. "He could never explain cartoons to you. And you don't understand them by yourself."

"Yeah, but that old frying pan wouldn't know how to have rubber duck races in the tub."

"Right again," Dad had to admit. "And then in the evening when it was time for a bath, I would have to ask the frying pan whether he wanted to

33

hop in the tub."

"That's true!" nodded Dad. "If there was no you, I would have no one to tell bedtime stories to, or do you think the box of cornflakes would enjoy them?"

"No!" said the boy. "And the cornflakes wouldn't hug you to say thank you for the wonderful story, would they?"

"No, and after the story I wouldn't have anybody to snuggle with," said Dad sadly. "I would have to try the bucket."

"That bucket is stinky," said the boy. "Besides, he wouldn't tug on your ear and say I love you!"

"That would be awful! And in the end I would have to put my newspaper to bed, tuck it in and wish it sweet dreams."

"And what about the goodnight kiss?" said the boy. "You couldn't get that from the newspaper."

"You're absolutely right," said Dad. "I really don't know what I would do without you. If there was no you, the whole day would be terribly sad and empty!"

"And I don't know, what I'd do without you either," said the boy. "It would sure be boring if there was no us. It's a good thing we're together!"

"Look, the moon is only half a honey-comb now," said the old bear on the next evening. "The sky-bears already ate the other half."

"There's no such thing as sky-bears," said the angel. "And the moon is made stone. You'd break your teeth if you tried to eat it."

"Aha," said the old bear. "And what about the stars?"
"Some stars are small suns and some are planets like the earth," explained the little angel. "And there are a lot of them. Some constellations even have names. Over there is an example… the small bear!"

"I knew that!" the old bear said, "and I also know a story."
So the old bear began the seventh story…

The Shaggy Bear *by Waltraud Egitz*

A little bear strained and stretched and squinted towards the sun. What a beautiful day! He pulled a few leaves from his fur and was off to find a few raspberries to pick for breakfast.
The little bear wanted to begin right away, when he heard a rustling sound. He sat very still and listened. Could it be that its friend Eddie was here?

Suddenly a head appeared from the forest of leaves. But it couldn't be Eddie's head because he had a head with silky smooth fur. The fur of this creature was shaggy! The little bear had never seen such a thing. No, this creature, this shaggy bear did not belong here. What could it possibly want here? The little bear straightened up as tall as he could and roared, "You can't come here!"

"AAAAAH!" said the shaggy bear, so frightened it ran away.
The little bear was quite satisfied with himself; the intruder was gone!
But what if he came back?
"I'll just have to hunt it," said the little bear as he began following the tracks of the strange shaggy bear. But at the brook he got lost.
"Where could that shaggy thing be hiding?" growled the little bear angrily.
He asked the crow, "Did a shaggy bear pass this way?"

"What kind of bear?" the crow asked.
"A really ugly, shaggy one," explained the little bear.

"Caw," said the crow. "Whether smooth or shaggy, a bear is a bear!"
"But the shaggy one doesn't belong here," said the little bear.

"Caw! And only because it is new here, you want to hunt it?" the crow asked. "Get to know him first, then you can decide whether or not you like him."

The little bear trotted off, thinking. He hadn't gone a hundred steps, when suddenly he was standing before a cave. And in front of the entrance was the strange bear with the shaggy fur sitting with large honey pot. The little bear stepped closer and saw that the shaggy bear was stirring crunchy nuts into the golden honey.

"What are you doing?" he asked. But the shaggy bear only peeked at him and didn't say a word.

The little bear knew why. "You're mad at me because I chased you, aren't you?" he asked.

"I'm not mad, just sad," said the shaggy bear. "I didn't do anything to you at all."
"Please don't be sad anymore," the little bear said and stuck out his paw.
"I'm the little bear, by the way."
"I'm Tino," said the shaggy bear.
"Tino," repeated the little bear. "Tell me why you are stirring nuts in the honey?"

"The honey tastes much better that way," said Tino. "My grandmother also adds raspberries sometimes. But I don't have any."
The little bear's mouth was beginning to water. He jumped up and took Tino by the paw.

"Come on, we're going raspberries picking… together!"

39

39

Evening 8

"Oh," yawned the little angel. "Today it will be really hard to stay awake. I am so tired!"

"Do you really sit up the whole night beside the child?" the bear asked.

"Yep, until the sun comes up," said the angel. "Then I creep into my cloud-bed and sleep a little." He snuggled in the grass. "Tell me a good night story," said the little angel.

"No, no," laughed the old bear. "Today it's your turn and I want to hear a good morning, stay-awake story."

The angel twisted and turned the little star on his cap. "Hmm... a wake up story. Oh, I've got it."

And the little angel began the eighth story....

Wake Up *by Catherine Metzmeyer*

"Kuckuck! Kuckuck!" came a loud call from the forest. The two little bears in their big dark cave woke up with a start. Outside the fresh grass was growing, soft and green. The little bears were so excited they made somersaults and sang, "Mama, Papa, it's time to wake up, spring is here!"
But their parents just kept sleeping.

"Get up, get up!"
"It's time to get up!"
"Hurry and get up, we're hungry!"

The two little bears made so much noise that all neighbors came running. Together they shook Mama and Papa Bear. But it seemed nothing could be done. From under his moss blanket Papa Bear just growled and Mama Bear opened her eyes but then closed them again.

Can you imagine!
The hedgehog tried a little poke using one of his prickly spines—nothing!
The woodpecker tried poking with his bill—still nothing.
Papa and Mama Bear just kept on snoring.
"Just let them sleep," said the snail. "When it's time, they'll wake up."

But the others didn't give up.

"Now it's my turn," said the squirrel. "Just a little tickle and they'll wake up, guaranteed!" And he wiggled his bushy tail, back and forth, under their noses, even in their noses....
Mama Bear sneezed a lady-like sneeze.
"HAAAA-CHOOOO!" roared Papa Bear. Both bears pulled their blankets up over their noses and kept sleeping.
"I never knew waking up could be so difficult," said the squirrel.

"Booo," screamed the first little bear. "Rooaar!" tried the second. Still nothing. No matter what they tried, their parents just kept sleeping.

41

The snail twitched with her feelers. "Just wait!" she said. But nobody seemed to hear.

"I have an idea," said the rabbit suddenly. "Come, children," and all the rabbit children hopped up on the bear's bed. They even did somersaults. But it didn't help. Mama and Papa Bear just kept sleeping. The two little bears didn't know what to do. They were ready to cry. What if their parents didn't wake up?

At that very moment a tiny little sunbeam shone into the cave through the door. It touched the thick pillow of fern and tickled Papa Bear's cheek and then touched Mama Bear's eyelids. Both the bear parents suddenly jumped out of bed.

"Get up, get up," said Papa Bear.
"Everybody, wake up!" called Mama Bear. "It's time!"
"Yippee!" cried the little bears happily. "Winter is over!"
"Good morning," sang all animals. "It's spring!"

And while the rooster spread the good news throughout the forest, the little snail mumbled, "I knew it all along," and since it was time for her midday nap she crawled back into her little house and fell fast asleep.

43

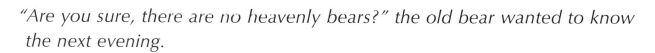

Evening 9

"Are you sure, there are no heavenly bears?" the old bear wanted to know the next evening.

"I'm sure," said the little angel. "Though outer space is so amazingly super- duper-enormous, perhaps one might find a place to hide in a far away corner somewhere."

The old bear nodded and asked, "And what about little white elephants?"

"Oh, thunder claps and lightening bolts! No,"
said the angel. "There are no heavenly elephants,
not white or green, not even striped!
Why do you want to know?"
"Because there is a story about them," said the bear,
and so began the ninth story.

The Little White Elephant

by Heinz Janisch

Once when old Oscar was sad, he happened to meet Sam on the bridge.
Sam sensed right away that something was bothering Oscar.
He gave Oscar the shoebox he was carrying and said, "Inside is my little
white elephant. He will look after you. Give him something to eat and
drink and please put him by an open window at night. He likes that. He
thinks every star in the sky is a little white elephant!"

The old man was a bit surprised, but carried the box happily home. He
announced to the table and chair, to the bed and to the window, "We have
a visitor tonight, a little white elephant will be staying over."

Before it was dark, Oscar took the little white elephant out of the box. It
was beautiful and stood quite still as if it were made of stone. It wasn't
hungry and it wasn't thirsty. So, Oscar opened the window and looked for
prettiest spot on the windowsill. From there the little white elephant would
be able to see the stars—the whole white shimmering herd!

Oscar sat down. "So, little friend," he said, "what are you thinking about?"
But the little elephant wasn't in the mood to talk. He stood very still and
looked at the sky. Oscar glanced up at the stars as well and he realized
that it was he who had so many thoughts going through his head. He
thought of all the people that he had known over his many years…
Suddenly the old man saw so many faces before him that he had to close
his eyes for a moment. "I see so many friends," he said to the white
elephant. "Look at that star over there, that's Maria, there is Marco, and
there is Jim…"

The whole night Oscar told the little elephant stories about life and friend-
ship, coming and going away, about laughter and sadness.
The old man didn't fall asleep until it was light, and then he slept until noon.
He gave the little elephant something to eat and drink and then laid him on   45

his bed of straw. As he carried the shoebox to the bridge, he met Sam. "Thank you," said Oscar. "We had a wonderful time together. We looked at the stars together, and after a while there seemed to be so much to say. I know now that I still have friends, not only in my memories, but here in town. I'm going to visit a few of them. You can come visit me too, now that we're friends."

"We will," said Sam, "but today I want to show my little white elephant the sea!" Oscar thought a moment. He said, "The sea is too far away, I'm afraid."

"Oh we're just going to start with the pond over there," said Sam.
Oscar nodded and then Sam nodded too, and they both started off.

47

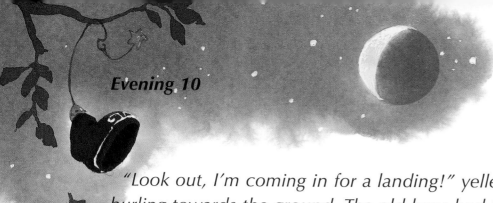

"Look out, I'm coming in for a landing!" yelled the little angel as he came hurling towards the ground. The old bear had just come out of the forest. Shocked, he jumped out of the way just in the nick of time.

"Excuse me," mumbled the angel while he tried to recover from his landing. "I guess I need some more practice!"

"It's okay," said the old bear. "But, hey, look at the red plums hanging on the tree over there. I've never seen them like that before."

"That's my cap, silly," laughed the angel and fluttered up to get it. "But that does remind me of a story." And so the little angel began telling the tenth story.

Joseph and the Plum Tree

by Brigitte Weninger

There was a little path that led away from the village street and up the hill. Joseph's house was at the top of the hill, and right next to it was a big old plum tree. In the past there were often people from the village who came to talk to Joseph and buy the plums. But the tree got older, and there wasn't as much fruit. "See, they don't need us anymore," said Joseph.

"No plums, no visitors. Then that's the way it will be!" said Joseph.
The tree creaked and groaned as if to answer.
Joseph seldom went down to the village after that, and as the years went by he became as gnarled and bent as his plum tree. Weeds and moss grew over the narrow path to the house until no one could see it any more.
On a late summer day, however, a little girl peeked over the fence.

"What do you want? Go away," growled Joseph. But Ilsa paid no attention and sat down next to him.
"Why is the path to your door all grown over?" she asked.
"Because no one comes to visit anymore," answered Joseph.
"And what about you, don't you ever use the path?" asked Ilsa.

"No, I don't go anywhere anymore!" he said.
"Then of course the moss will grow," nodded the girl.
Both sat very still.
Then suddenly Joseph began to tell how it was in earlier days, when both he and the plum tree were young. How it was when there were baskets of plums and the evening chats with people from the village. But that was long ago and plum time is over.

The girl listened carefully.
"You tell wonderful stories," she said. "Plum time isn't over. Look, there is one hanging on the tree. Can I have it?"
"I don't give them away, I eat them myself," mumbled the old man.

49

"Will you loan it to me?" asked Ilsa.

"Don't be ridiculous," said Joseph. "You can't loan plums."

Sure you can," said Ilsa mischievously as she hit the tree with Joseph's cane. She took a bite of the plum.

"Mmmm, it is so sweet!" she said.

"So, what about the 'loaning?'" asked Joseph.

Ilsa laid the plum seed in Joseph hand.

"Here," she said. "You gave part of the plum to me and I'm giving part of the plum back to you. That's the loan, and I think you got the better part of the deal, because from the seed a new tree can grow!"

"That's true," said Joseph, thinking back to a time long ago. "I planted that tree myself when I was about your age…"

"You see," said Ilsa, rather satisfied with herself. "Then good night, Joseph, and I'll come again tomorrow and you can tell me a new story."

That evening Joseph didn't grumble and mumble as he usually did. No, he whistled a tune. It was a song his mother had often sung to him which reminded him of one of her old fairy tales.

"That's what I'll tell Ilsa tomorrow," thought Joseph. "And perhaps I'll visit the village again and bring Ilsa a little present."

Smiling, Joseph put the little plum seed in flower pot and covered it with warm soil.

50

Evening 11

The next evening the little angel stood hiding something behind his back.
"Guess which hand!" he said to the bear. "If you can guess and guess it right,
  it's yours to keep this very night."
"Which hand could it be? Left or right or right or left?" asked the bear.
"I think it's in your… left hand!"
You're right!" said the angel and handed the bear a beautiful little round box.
"Oh, thank you," said the bear, a bit confused. "Why are you giving me a present?"
"Just because," laughed the little angel. "But you can't open it until I say so,
  and before you do I would like to hear another story." So the bear began the
  eleventh story.

52

Andrew's Present *by Franz Noser*

It was Sunday morning. Everyone was still asleep, except Andrew. He had found the wrapping paper box. He was very nosey.

"The red paper with the stars and moons is great." he said. "I would wrap a present in that, but I don't have anything to wrap." Andrew thought and thought. "I could wrap up Laura's stuffed dog. I'm sure she doesn't need it anymore."

But Laura was not happy. "That's mine!" she said, "You can't have it." Andrew ran to Mama and Papa's bedroom. They were still in bed and little Adam was asleep in his cradle.
"Laura won't give me her stuffed dog," snapped Andrew.

"What do you need it for?" asked Papa.
"I want to wrap a present," said Andrew. "I already have the paper."
"I see, and who is the present for?" continued Papa.
"I don't know yet," said Andrew.

Mama said, "That's not the way with presents. You don't start with the paper, then pick out the present and then find someone to give it to. You've got it a bit backwards."

"No," said Andrew, pouting. "You can do it my way too!"
Papa had an idea. "What if you give your slingshot away as a gift?" he said. "I know your piggybank would be happy when that slingshot was no longer in your room!"
"No," said Andrew. "My slingshot is too small for my wrapping paper."
"What about some bubble gum?" asked Laura.
"No, that's even smaller."

"Why don't you wrap up your tin drum?" asked Mama.
"Uncle Fred gave that to me!" cried Andrew. "You don't understand anything about presents!"
Andrew grabbed the wrapping paper and stomped off to his room.   53

He lay on his bed and looked at the paper just like Papa did when he read the newspaper.

"The wrapping paper looks like a piece of the sky full of stars," he thought. "Too bad I can't fly there. Hey, that's a great idea, I'll build a rocket!"

Andrew found an empty toilet paper roll, scissors, cardboard and glue. He cut and glued, he colored and decorated, and at the end he drew two astronauts in the cockpit. One astronaut was named Andrew and the other was... Dougie, his friend from kindergarten. And suddenly Andrew knew exactly who the present was for!

He wrapped the present very carefully, put a ribbon around it and took it with him to kindergarten.

"This is for you," Andrew said when he saw his friend. Dougie opened it and said, "Hey, a rocket!" He was so excited he jumped up shouting, "Thank you! Why don't you come over today and we can play space travelers."

Andrew was happy that Dougie liked his present. Andrew carefully smoothed out the wrinkles and crinkles from the wrapping paper.

"Sure, and I'll bring outer space," he said, waving the star-covered paper.

"Sorry, I had to fly off last night so suddenly," said the little angel. "And you still don't know what's in the little round box."

"Oh, that's okay," said the old bear. "It's kind of fun waiting for something special. I've been thinking about it and perhaps the little round box itself is the present—like the star paper in your story."

"You are such a clever bear," said the little angel. "Do you want to have a peek?"

"No, I'd rather hear a gift story," said the old bear, laughing. The little angel began the twelfth story.

56

A Birthday Sausage for Piccolo

by Ute Messner

Woof, woof! I'm Piccolo, Granny Paloma's favorite dog. My fur is brown and black and white and I'm a little bit cross-eyed, but Granny Paloma always says, "Good dog, pretty dog!" when she pets me.

I like it when she pets me, and Flo does too. Flo is my pet flea and my friend. During the day we protect our house and the yard and at night we sleep on our blanket in the hall. Today Flo and I celebrate "our" birthday. Every year we get a sausage! Last year we got two sausages, and that's a fact! I have a very good sausage memory.

And Granny Paloma makes a cake! That's Flo's favorite thing (he loves rolling in the frosting). Personally I would prefer a cake with sausages on top, but Granny Paloma says, "No, candles belong on top, you can't blow out sausages to make a wish." Since today is our birthday we are allowed to go out into the wide, wide world. So we're going to the zoo, right around the corner.

First we go to The World of Ice—it's really cold. Our penguin friends, Ping, Pong and Peng waddle over and sing Happy Birthday to us in the South Pole penguin language. They dance around us on the ice too.
"Here's your birthday gift," says Ping. "It's a ball of ice—Happy Birthday!"

Then Flo and I go to the Water Park. Our dolphin friends, Flipp, Flopp and Flupp can jump so high. They jump out of the water and spin in the air and call out "Happy Birthday! Catch your present!" It is also a little ball, with lots of colors. "See you soon!" they shout.
I can't answer because I have two balls in my mouth.

We are off to Jungle Land. Wow, it's like a barrel full of monkeys! Sure enough, we see our three monkey friends, Tang, Kekey and Gori swinging in the trees and singing, Happy Birthday!

"Here's your present," they sing all together and toss a yellow sausage down,   57

right in front of my paws. I take a bite,
but it's sweet and gooshy.

"That's not a sausage," Flo says, laughing. "It's a banana! Yum,
I like bananas."
Suddenly we hear a voice shouting, "Piccolo, Piii-co-looo!"
It's Granny Paloma. It's time to go home. I want to take my gifts with me,
but I can only find the little ball. What happened to the ice ball?

At home Granny Paloma is waiting for us with a cake with three candles.
We blow them out and make a wish. Flo wriggles around in the frosting,
and Granny Paloma pets me and says, "Good dog, pretty dog!"
Flo and I are happy, but we're dog-tired and start towards our blanket in
the hall.

"That's strange," I say. "Last year we got two sausages, I'm sure of it. I have
a very good sausage memory. Why did we get three sausages this year?"

"Because every year for our birthday we get one more sausage," says Flo.

"Hey that's right," I say. "Bow wow! That means we are three sausages old!
Next birthday we'll be four sausages old, and when we're a hundred, that
means we'll be 100 sausages old. What a birthday party that'll be, I can
hardly wait! That's definitely something to dream about…
Woof, woof!"

58

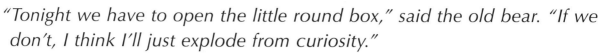

"Tonight we have to open the little round box," said the old bear. "If we don't, I think I'll just explode from curiosity."
Their two heads bent over the little container as they opened it together.
"I knew it, it's empty!" roared the old bear. "It's empty!"

"That's not true!" said the little angel. "There's something lovely inside, but it's invisible. Why, this is a comfort-box! When you worry or have a problem, you just put it in here. That way you'll sleep peacefully. In the morning when you peek in, you'll find your 'comfort,' and you'll know that things will be just fine.
"What a wonderful present, thank you!" said the bear. "Too bad Fiona didn't have a little comfort-box."
And the old bear started the thirteenth story.

60

The Monster Mouse

by Brigitte Weninger

Fiona and Mama were walking through the department store. Suddenly Fiona saw something that she had been wanting for a long time. It was a stuffed mouse that could actually run and make a cute little "peep-peep" sound.

"Look, Mama," said Fiona, "it's just what I want."
"That's nice dear," said Mama. "Let's put that on your birthday wish list."

"No," said Fiona. "I want it now."
"I don't buy toys every time we go shopping," said Mama firmly. "Now let's go." But Fiona didn't budge. When Mama went to the cashier, Fiona took the mouse off the shelf and put it in her pocket.

When they got home Fiona ran straight to her room. She took out the mouse and pushed its start button and let the mouse run all over the room. But its peep-peep voice was much too loud. What if Mama came to her room? Fiona quickly turned off the mouse and put it back in her pocket

When Mama called her for lunch, Fiona was not hungry. She kept thinking she heard the "peep-peep." She had to check. No, it was quite still, but Fiona had the feeling that the mouse had somehow gotten bigger, much bigger. It didn't fit in her pocket anymore. The ears and tail were sticking out.

"I need a new hiding place for the mouse," said Fiona. "But where? I've got it—in the toy-box!"
She cleaned out all the toys and put the not-so-little mouse in. But there was no longer room for all the other toys. She just left them where they were and ran out to the back yard. But swinging wasn't any fun today. She kept thinking about the mouse. What if Mama looked in the toy box? Fiona needed a better hiding place, maybe the closet!

And sure enough when Fiona was ready to move the mouse it had gotten even bigger. She had to pull out all her sweaters to make space for the mouse.

"This isn't going to work either," said Fiona. "I need a better hiding place." She took the mouse out of the closet and was thinking about a better hiding place when her mother came into the room. Fiona had just enough time to shove the mouse under the bed.

"It's time for bed," said her mother smiling. "You can clean your room up in the morning." Fiona nodded and thought sadly that she would have to do it all alone, so that Mama wouldn't find the mouse.

After Mama had kissed her goodnight, Fiona was unable to sleep. She thought about playing with the mouse, but she really didn't want to. Then... What was that? Help!

Did the bed just move? Had she felt a wiggle? Maybe the mouse was growing even bigger!

Perhaps it wasn't a stuffed mouse after all, but a monster mouse that would grow as big as her room or as big as the house... Fiona jumped out of bed and ran to her mother's room.

"Mama, wake up! I have something to tell you!" cried Fiona.

Fiona was trembling and her mother held her tightly and listened as Fiona explained everything about the monster mouse.

"I'm glad you told me everything," said Mama. "We'll take care of it tomorrow. Now we should get some sleep."

The next morning Fiona and Mama looked carefully under the bed.

"That's funny," said Fiona. "The mouse is little again. Why, he doesn't even look scary. But you know what, Mama? I still want to take it back to the store."

And with that, Mama gave
Fiona a big hug and kiss!

Evening 14
New Moon

"From today on we'll be sitting in the dark," said the old bear on the following evening. "The beautiful honey colored moon is gone."
"No, it's not," said the little angel. "The moon is still there, you just can't see it! Soon a thin little sliver will appear and then we will start from the beginning again. Every night the moon will get rounder. You know what the humans used to say? They said what one started at the new moon was easiest to accomplish!"

"Well, that's good to know!" said the bear.
"Then beginning tonight I'll stop eating so many treats."
"And I'll really start practicing," said the little angel.
"But before I start, I have a very nice story for you!"
And the little angel told the fourteenth story.

Closed Today *by Jan C. Schliephack*

On Tuesday the tulip didn't feel very well. It had rained all night and now it
felt cold, especially around the stem.
"Today I think I will stay closed," it said.

"What's the matter?" asked a bumble bee.
"I'm closed," said the tulip.
"That's strange," said a second bee. "I wonder why the tulip won't open."

"Because I'm closed," said the tulip.
"Well, imagine that," the bumble bee grumbled as he flew away.
 The maybug had no luck either. "What's the matter?" he asked.
"Closed!" said the tulip, feeling rather snippy. It was getting to be just too much.
 And so the whole day long, no matter who came, the tulip's petals stayed closed.

"The tulip is really acting strangely," said the bumble bee.
"If you ask me," said the butterfly, "it's crazy! Total nonsense!"
"Inexcusable," said the maybug.
 They were all very upset!

"We'd better do something," said the hungry bumblebees. "Maybe we should
 shake her till she opens up!"

"Let's just tickle her. Sooner or later she'll have to open up," said the butterfly.

"What if we all sit on her at once?" suggested the fly.
"Don't be silly," said an impatient wasp. "We'll just hang on good and tight
 and then all poke together!"

 Only the little ladybug had said nothing. But now her squeaky little voice
 came from one of the tulip petals.
"No, we won't do anything to her." she said. "Haven't you noticed that after the
 rain she looks more wonderful than ever, and her scent... delicious?"
 They all looked at the tulip.   65

"I'm closed today," said the tulip. She was getting rather annoyed. "Don't you understand?"

The maybug flew up to one of the petals and sighed, "Oh, and the fragrance is so wonderful and yummy!"
The others circled around the tulip. "She positively glows," said the butterfly. "Like a queen!"
"Your stem it so slender and fine," whispered the ladybug to the tulip.

"Your petals are smooth with tiny water beads, like they have pearls on them. You are like an ornament, a decoration for the whole meadow," said the dragonfly, who was quite beautiful herself.

"Your fragrance is so sweet, I can't sleep at night," said a bumblebee rubbing his delicate feelers on one of her leaves.

And so it continued, for almost a half an hour, one lovely compliment after another. The tulip couldn't believe it—a warm feeling came over her and she blushed. She swayed lightly in the wind. Maybe the day wasn't so bad after all, and what lovely things they all had to say.

Finally, the tulip sighed softly, and with that her petals gently opened.

Evening 15

"Unbelievable! What a scene there was last night," explained the little guardian angel. "The child didn't want to go to bed. As a matter of fact, he had quite a tantrum. I had no idea that child knew so many naughty words! There were a few that even I had never heard, for example…"

"Stop, stop," said the old bear. "I don't want to know. Think about your Angel-eze. You're supposed to learn to speak like the big angels. I think it's better if I tell you a tantrum story."
And so the bear began story number fifteen.

68

Terrible Toby *by Karl Rühmann*

Sometimes Toby got angry with his parents. For example, when he wanted a special toy, one that would be really fun to play with, and his parents said no! His parents always liked a different toy, calling it "educational." But Toby thought those toys were dumb. It was very upsetting.

Once, for example, Toby really wanted french fries for lunch. But there was vegetable casserole instead!
"Yuck," complained Toby. "I'm not eating this junk!"
"Then just leave it," said his mother. "We're enjoying it!"
Toby was very angry and ran from the table. The whole afternoon he was hungry. "Maybe that dumb casserole wouldn't have been so bad," thought Toby as he heard his stomach growling.

Later Toby had to go to the barber. He hated getting his hair cut because it always felt so prickly when it was short. Luckily, Dad had to talk to Mr. Peterson and wasn't paying attention. That was Toby's chance to run, but Dad was faster. He took Toby home and cut Toby's hair himself. Toby was furious when he looked in the mirror. "I look like a plucked canary," he thought. "It would have been better if the hairdresser had done it!" Now it was too late!

That evening Toby was putting the finishing touches on the castle he was building.
He only had to attach the drawbridge, so the robbers couldn't get in.
"Time for bed," said Dad. "You can finish your castle in the morning."
"And what about the robbers?" Toby was so mad he picked up the whole castle and threw it against the wall.
Crash! Now there was much more than just the draw bridge to finish and it would be even easier for the robbers to get in.

The next day didn't begin any better. "Toby," said his mother at breakfast.
"We're not going to the seashore this summer, it's just too expensive, but we'll have a lot of fun here at home."

What? Fun? Here? No way! Now Toby was really mad;
how could they do that to him? "But I want to build
sandcastles, go swimming and collect shells!"
he screamed. He threw a chair, slammed the door
behindhim and ran. Toby saw the big tree next to
the house. He climbed up quickly and hid. Soon Mom
and Dad came out of the house. "Tooooby, Toby!"
they called and called. They looked everywhere for him.

"Toby, where are you? Please come back."
Toby watched from his hiding place. He knew they'd
never find him in the tree. They kept calling and calling.
He felt a little sorry for them.

They looked so small from up in the tree. His anger
seemed to get smaller and smaller too. Then it was
gone! Toby climbed down out of the tree and ran to
his parents. He remembered that there was a big
sandbox near the swimming pool, and he already
had too many seashells!
Toby still gets angry sometimes but every time
he starts to get angry, he remembers the tree.
From up high in the tree everything looked
small... even his anger!

The next evening a voice from the clouds said, "Look!"
The old bear looked but couldn't see anything. Suddenly the little angel appeared.
"Look how I'm flying!" he shouted from far away. "And now watch me land!"
He fluttered his wings, started getting slower—and crashed! The big bear caught him easily with his strong paws.
"Oh, phooey, not again," said the little angel. "And I was flying so well!"

"I saw you," said the bear, fibbing a little. "Now you only have to practice those landings and you get an A-Number-1 on your guardian angel test."

"And soon!" said the little angel all excited. "But first I have a spooky-creepy story for you."
The little angel began story sixteen!

72

Reginald, the Fearless *by Brigitte Weninger*

Sir Reginald was a knight and lived all alone in his castle high up in a valley. The castle was not large, but neither was Sir Reginald. He had never been out in the big wide world because he always got sick when he traveled. He had never saved a princess from a dragon because he couldn't stand the smell of stinky, unwashed dragon feet.

He didn't even have honorable battle wounds to show. Well, he had one on his behind, but he couldn't very well show that and so he had no found no lady who wanted to be the damsel for his castle. He had dreamed of it often, though.

One evening someone knocked on the castle door. "Now who could that be?" wondered Sir Reginald. "Maybe a pretty damsel in distress! I could rescue her and then we could marry and have seventeen children!" Excited he opened the door and saw a beautiful white dress.

But attached to the upper part of the dress smiled a spooky-creepy ghost face. It howled with ghostly hollow voice, "I am Argus the Awful and from tonight on, I'm going to haunt your castle. So get going you creepy little creature before I give you a good swift kick."

"Bu… bu… bu... But this is MY castle!" stuttered Sir Reginald, completely confused.
"What?" hollered the ghost. "You don't want me to… Well, then!"
The ghost grew bigger and bigger before Sir Reginald's very eyes, until it was bigger that the tower and wailed so loudly. It sounded like a fire alarm with a stomachache.

Poor Sir Reginald was so shocked he flipped the visor of his armor closed. Unfortunately, he forgot that his nose didn't quite fit. As the visor pinched his nose, Sir Reginald screamed like two fire alarms with stomachaches.

The ghost was so shocked, but then it continued howling, "Haven't you had enough?" He pointed with his spindly ghost fingers and a terrible storm suddenly erupted. The thunder and lightning was so strong that it made the walls shake. Then the rain came down in buckets!

Sir Reginald knew exactly what would happen, and sure enough, his suit of armor rusted so quickly that he couldn't move at all.
The little knight swayed squeakily forward and from side to side in the wind moving forward, always forward and straight toward the ghost.
"He is brave, braver than I thought," said the ghost.
"There is only one thing left to try, and if that doesn't work, I'll have to find another castle."

Argus grunted and flung himself towards Sir Reginald, hoping to tickle him to death. But the suit of armor wouldn't budge. In the end the ghost gave up, disappearing into the night, and wailing the most pitiful wail.

The next morning it was the village barber who found the "rusted" Sir Reginald and went immediately to get a can opener. He opened the rusty armor, freeing the poor knight. The barber was not only the first to find Sir Reginald, but the first to hear Sir Reginald's story of the battle with Argus the Awful. Oddly the barber didn't hear the part about Sir Reginald's smashed nose or how his armor got so rusty…
Could it be that Sir Reginald the Fearless forgot to mention it?

74

"I brought something for you," said the old bear and handed it to the
little angel.
"That's nice," said the angel. "What is it?"
"An extra-big honey bread," said the bear. "I fixed it myself!"

"How thoughtful," said the angel. "The only thing is, angels don't eat. We
need only air and love."
"Now isn't that interesting," said the bear. "But what should we do with the
lovely honey bread?"
"I would like to give it to my very best friend," said the angel. "Then he can
tell me a story."
"What a yummy idea," said the bear. "I know just the story…"
And with his lips smacking loudly, the bear start the seventeenth story.

The Big Smacker! *by Géraldine Elschner*

Georgie was known in his family for one thing. Whatever he put in his mouth to eat, he smacked his lips so loudly that no one could stand it. He would heap piles of food on a piece of bread. No matter how much Georgie piled on, he was a master, and he'd open up wide enough to get it all in his mouth. Then he'd sit back and enjoy, chomping, smacking, and noisily savoring every chewy chomp.

"Honey, don't chew like that, it's so loud," said his mother, sighing.
"This is not a barn," scolded his father.
But Georgie just gulped and swallowed, "It's so yummy! Aren't you hungry?"
The others had lost their appetites.

On the way to school he didn't smack. He chewed, but like a cow in the meadow, sticking in one piece of gum after the other. He also chewed on the end of his pencil in class, just like a hungry beaver. And every evening the smacking would start all over again.
"Would you quit it, you're so loud, I can't stand it!" screamed his sister.
"Georgie, the Giant Smacker!" Everyone laughed, except George.

He went sadly to bed, falling asleep with his thumb in his mouth. He was very quiet and didn't snore.
One Sunday when his grandparents were visiting, something awful happened. His mother had set a beautiful table. His father had bought a special bottle of wine, and they were all were sitting at the table.

For this special meal his mother had prepared a special appetizer…
"Real snails from France!" his mother said proudly.
"Yuk!" shouted Georgie.
"Quiet," ordered his father.
George really didn't want to make a scene, so he tried slurping on the snail shell and chewed much longer than usual and also much louder. But it was as if he had a piece of car tire in his mouth. So he chewed and

77

smacked to the left, and then he chewed and smacked to the right, because the snail was stuck between his teeth. They all just stared at him. But Georgie was deep in thought, so he didn't notice everyone looking at him angrily. He kept thinking about the poor snails, living in the woods. It was certainly a nice life under the trees, in the rain... He lifted his head almost teary-eyed and saw everyone starring at him.

"That's enough. GO TO YOUR ROOM, THIS MINUTE!" exploded his father. Georgie burst into tears and ran to his room. He lay sobbing a long time before the door opened...
"George, may I come in?" It was his grandmother.

"I prefer snails better in the woods than on a plate, any day," she said. "I told them that, too! Now...look what I've brought for you."
"What, you mean a present?" George was still sniffling but he pushed away the covers. He opened the colorful cover and took out a beautiful harmonica. It shone like a mirror. He stuck it immediately in his mouth.

"Slowly," laughed his grandmother. "Watch, back straight, lips closed and then..."
And that's how it all started.
First Georgie learned to play the harmonica. Then it was the clarinet, trumpet and saxophone. Anything that he could get between his teeth, but he was no longer a noisy eater! He played so well and made such beautiful music that he eventually became famous all over the world.
He had a funny nickname, though.
He was called the Giant Smacker!
How he got that nickname, nobody knows...
Well, almost nobody.

79

Evening 18

"You can't imagine what happened last night," said the little angel, his voice still sounding rather shaky. "I was sitting next to the child and was whispering the special word, when suddenly a cat came in through the balcony door. It wanted to grab me! Can you imagine? I flew up toward the ceiling and got away. I thought all cats were as nice as Nala."

The old bear gave the little angel a hug.
"Don't be mad at the cat. It probably thought you were a bird. Tell me about this Nala. Does it belong to the child?"
"No, but it lives in the same building," said the little angel,
                    and at once he knew the eighteenth story…

80

The Cat in the Stairwell

by Bruno Hächler

Nala stood on the stairs and listened. In the last rays of sunlight, her fur shone red. Nala waited till it was dark and then crept down the stairs.

Every evening Nala roamed up and down the stairwell. She loved the wooden stairs and the little corners and spaces. She loved shoes by the doors best of all. She sniffed at the buckles and soles, rubbed against the soft leather or played with the untied laces. It was not unusual for the people to find everything turned upside down in front of the doors.
They would just laugh and say, "That's Nala!" They all liked the little cat.

Once when Nala went outside to check the garden, a black tomcat appeared from out of nowhere. He hissed and showed his claws. Like an arrow Nala flew out of the garden and back in the building. Since then she has stayed in the stairwell.

Step by step Nala crept down the stairs. She stopped by a door on the first floor. The door was open a crack. Nala couldn't resist and slid silently into the apartment.
It was full of furniture, books and plants. There were toys everywhere. Nala looked in every direction, deciding which room to visit first. She moved down the long hall and disappeared into the kitchen.

In the kitchen it was almost dark. Everything smelled new and secretive. Nala sniffed, looked and then perked up her ears.
She heard a noise coming from the hall.
Tap, tap, tap.
The noise came closer.
Tap, tap, tap.
The fur on Nala neck stood up. She wanted to run away but she didn't know where to run.
The way out of the kitchen was blocked and there was no other way to go.   81

Tap, tap, tap.
Nala fled under a cupboard full of cans. From the
sliver of light that came in the kitchen there
appeared a spooky shadow. It kept getting bigger.
It was a tomcat shadow with teeth and claws.
Nala made herself as flat as possible on the
floor. She was almost invisible.

TAP, TAP, TAP, TAP!
The light went on and standing in the kitchen door
was a little girl with freckles and messy hair.
She didn't look dangerous at all.

"Nala, what are you doing in here?" she asked.
Nala didn't move.

"Don't be afraid! My name is Sophie.
I live here."
Slowly Sophie moved towards Nala and then
stuck out her hand and pet Nala on the head.
Nala was afraid at first, but then she liked it.
She liked Sophie. Soon Nala was purring and
when Sophie stopped petting, Nala pressed
her head in Sophie's hand and rubbed against her.
They sat together until Sophie got tired.

"You should stay here with me tonight,"
said Sophie, yawning.
She gently picked Nala up and carried her
to her room and they snuggled together
deep down under the covers.
Good Night, little Nala!

"Do you remember the story about the cat in the stairwell from yesterday?" asked the little angel. "Of course," nodded the bear.

"Well, it occurred to me," said the little angel, "that it's hard to tell what is happening on the inside, by just looking at the outside. Some look sweet and nice but really aren't. Others look dangerous but are really gentle. Then there are those who are sometimes one way and sometimes the other. How are we ever supposed to know?"

"It's best to decide by looking at each situation as they come," said the old bear. "I have a story for tonight that might help," and the bear began the nineteenth story.

84

Tiger in the Mirror *by Peter Norden*

Plop! It had happened again. Munkel was so shocked that he ran and actually somersaulted down the stairs.

"Did you see that?" giggled the mice from their hiding place. "Just a little rustling noise and that scaredy-cat goes flying down the stairs. Hee Hee Hee!"

"What am I going to do?" thought Munkel. He took a moment to recover from his tumble and crept back to his family who lived in a shed behind the old villa. It was already dark and Munkel was even more afraid after dark than he was during the day.

"What happened?" asked his mother. But she knew. She knew when something had frightened him.

"Your fur is dirty and standing every which way like yesterday when you ran away from the rabbit," she said.

"Or like last week when the crow frightened you so badly that you crawled into a mole hole," said his father.

"I know, I know," he sighed. If only he could be as brave as his parents or his brother! Having a scaredy-cat in the family must be a difficult for the whole family. Munkel felt awful.

At dinner Munkel was very still and deep in his own thoughts. Finally he said good night and went to bed. He lay there brooding. "This has got to stop," he thought. "I don't want to be a scaredy-cat, but what can I do...?" He fell asleep and must have begun to dream, for he was suddenly in the attic of the old villa. It was dark except for the slivers of moonlight that came through the cracks in the roof.

From every nook and cranny came strange sounds and noises. Munkel didn't know what to do. All his fur was standing on end and his heart was pounding in his chest. Suddenly in the pale moonlight Munkel saw a big mirror. He saw himself in the mirror, but something was different. His paws were much bigger and somehow his head looked...wider. The stripes on his fur were

85

darker too! Munkel remembered something his father had once told him: "You'll see, our Munkel will be a real tiger one day!"

His grandmother had also once told him that there were real tigers living in a land far away.

"Tigers," she said, "are the largest cats in the world. They are careful and watchful and they are never afraid, not of anyone or anything!" Munkel wondered why he had suddenly thought about the tiger, but he made a decision. I won't ever forget the tiger in the mirror… I am the tiger in the mirror. He nodded to the tiger, turned and returned to his room. He felt something, a new kind of feeling.

Early the next morning Munkel woke up and felt an unusual prickly-tickly feeling. He threw off his blanket so he could look at himself. But he looked like he always did.

"Munkel, what are you going to do today?" asked his mother at breakfast.

"I thought I'd go play with the rabbit," said Munkel. "Then, I thought I'd go visit the crows up in their tree and maybe scare of few mice if I see any!" The whole family just stared at him.

"You must be dreaming!" said his father.

"I have been dreaming," giggled Munkel and snarled softly.

But is sounded like a real tiger growl!
It sounded like a real, grown up tiger growl.

Evening 20

On the next evening the crescent moon was so bright one could see every blade of grass.

"I found a four-leaf clover!" exclaimed the little angel and laid it in the old bear's paw.

"Thank you," said the bear and ate it right up!

"But… But… That was a good luck clover," said the angel.

"What? Oh, I didn't know," said the surprised bear.

"Well, I guess it doesn't matter, now you have the good luck in your tummy," giggled the little angel. "It reminds me of a funny good-luck story."

And that's how the angel began the twentieth story.

The Spaceship Lucky-Underpants *by Brigitte Weninger*

"Wow, I look great!" thought Freddy as he looked at himself in the mirror. Oinker, his stuffed pig, nodded. Freddy was wearing his super-duper space-ship underpants that Grandma had given him. Sometimes Grandma gave him really dumb presents, but the underpants were a hit. Honest to goodness, lucky underpants.

"Man, oh man, there are stars everywhere," said Freddy. "And look, where I sit, there's even an astronaut. You know, Oinker, when you wear these under-pants you can't help but feel like a real astronaut, real strong and brave!"

Oinker thought that was great because most of the time Freddy was a bit of "fraidy-cat." That's why he wanted to wear his lucky spaceship underpants all night. His mom gave him his teddy-bear pajamas instead.
"Oh, that's okay," Freddy whispered to Oinker. "I'll put them back on tomorrow in the morning and then watch out, I'll show 'em!"

It was still dark when Freddy woke up.
"The brave astronaut puts on his spacesuit," whispered Freddy and hopped in his clothes in the dark. Strange—today he wasn't afraid that there were ghosts staring at him. That was, of course, because he was wearing his lucky underpants.

Then Freddy took Oinker and made his way down the hall. He saw light coming from the kitchen.

"Hey, what are you doing up?" said his father. "I was going to make breakfast but we don't have any bread."
Astronaut Freddy thought for a moment and said, "I can fly to the bakery!"

"What, you?" said his father. Normally Freddy wouldn't even go in the back-yard by himself.
"That would be great," said his father and gave Freddy the money. "I think it's   89

terrific that you're going to the bakery today!"

His father's praise made Freddy feel great. He had his lucky underpants to thank!

"Astronaut Freddy and his friend Oinker exploring a new planet," Freddy mumbled as went down the quiet street. It didn't stay that way for long. Freddy and Oinker went by Mrs. Woodson's house and a giant black dog came running to the fence. "Grrrr, woof, bow-wow, grrr!" The dog always did that when Freddy walked by, and every time he did, Freddy's heart seemed to stop beating. But today he had on his lucky underpants.

Suddenly Freddy got angry. "Oh, leave me alone you fat, old dog!" he yelled. "Do you hear me? Quiet!" The big dog was so surprised that his tail went between his legs, and he was quiet.

"Did you see that, Oinker?" asked Freddy. "That monster did what I wanted! These lucky underpants are amazing!"
Astronaut Freddy flew on to the bakery.
"What a good boy you ar e to come and getbread this early," said the lady behind the counter as she gave him a lollipop.
"My favorite," he said. "Thank you!"
"Oinker, these underpants are unbelievable," Freddy said. "I'll just have to wear them every day!"
The two marched home happy as could be.

"Mission accomplished, Sir!" said Astronaut Freddy proudly.
His father took the bread and said,
"Thanks, big guy, well done!"
At that moment, Freddy's mother came out of his room carrying the dirty laundry and there was—no, it couldn't be...
There, right on the top were his Spaceship Lucky Underpants!

90

91

"In a couple of days the big yellow moon will be round again," said the old bear. "You will take the guardian angel test and will fly on, and I still won't know anything about the Special Word.

"Oh, phooey," said the little angel. "I forgot to ask if I could tell you. The Special word is a secret and only for Guardian Angels."

"But if it's soooo special, then everyone should know it, shouldn't they?" asked the bear.

"That's true," said the angel. "But I think I'd better check first, okay? I'll tell you a story about another special secret. How would that be?"
And so the little angel told the twenty-first story.

The Flying Mr. Zibrillo *by Heinz Janisch*

Mr. Zibrillo is an actor. He loves his job and his life on stage. He likes playing the marionette the best. He plays his role so well that sometimes after the performance he forgets to take off his strings. When the other actors are not working they go to a movie, a football game, or drive to the shore. But Mr. Zibrillo disappears into his workshop. Even as a little boy he had only one dream—he wanted to fly. Of course Mr. Zibrillo knows there are airplanes and helicopters, but Mr. Zibrillo wants to do it his own way.

"One day I'll lift off, just like that," he says, and he believes it. That's why every time he has a free minute, he builds the most unbelievable flying machines. In his workshop there is a bicycle with an open umbrella and a paper airplane so big that no one can throw it. There's an airplane seat with a built-in battery, a rowboat with wings and much, much more. Mr. Zibrillo is a very stubborn inventor. His inventions all look wonderful. The problem is, none of them work. The air mattress with the giant propeller and even the wonderful flying carpet that he wove himself just won't fly.

Mr. Zibrillo tries out all his inventions himself. He rolled down the steepest hill with his bike, rowed his boat up the river, placed his plane seat on the roof and turned on the battery. But nothing happened—Mr. Zibrillo didn't fly. One day Mr. Zibrillo decided to build a tweeter-machine, just because it was Sunday.

The tweeter-machine was so small he could put it in his pocket. Mr. Zibrillo took a walk in the meadow, stood in the tall grass and let the tweeter-machine tweet in his pocket. "What a pleasure," he thought as he closed his eyes and listened. How lovely it was, like the twittering and tweeting of birds! He felt so wonderful… and then it happened. Without realizing it himself, he lifted off! Slowly he lifted, two then three feet off the ground

He bent cautiously forward. How wonderfully light he was in the air! He stuck out his arms and moved them slowly. It worked!

93

While the tweeter-machine tweeted
and tweeted in his pocket, he flew. When
he got tired, he landed gently in the meadow, turned off the tweeter-machine and walked
home satisfied, whistling a tune.

The next afternoon Mr. Zibrillo was onstage playing the
role of a marionette. A new play was announced. Mr. Zibrillo
took the tweeter-machine out of his pocket and let it tweeter in the
theater. Then he released his marionette strings. He lifted higher and
higher in the air and flew over the heads of the surprised people in the
audience. The other actors released their strings and started floating, humming and laughing around the theater. Soon the audience was flying too, the
children and the adults, back and forth all over the auditorium. A flying
reporter wrote:

"What a sensation! One has to see it to believe it. Mr. Zibrillo has learned to fly!"
Late that evening Mr. Zibrillo took another walk. He grabbed the tweeter-
machine in his pocket.
94 "Just one more round," he said and lifted his arms.

95

"Look!" whispered the angel on the next evening. A little squirrel scampered to the nut tree.

"He's so little," said the bear. "Should he be allowed to run around by himself?"

"His guardian angel is with him," said the angel.

"I don't see anything," said the bear.

"Well, imagine what it would be like if with every person you saw, you saw their guardian angel. Why, your eyes would be covered with fuzzily-wuzzilies!"

"What are fuzzily wuzzilies?" asked the bear.

"Oh, forget it, that's just angel-eze. But don't forget that everyone has their guardian angel with them even when they are traveling alone, just like Alex…"

And the angel started the twenty-second story.

A Croissant to Snuggle *by Géraldine Elschner*

So what was missing?

Alex had been packing since noon. This year, for the first time, he was going to go with Aunt Lily to the shore, by himself, without Mom. Though his cousins would be there too, it was going to be great!

He looked in the closet. What else would he need? He really wanted to do this by himself; he was old enough.

"Let' see…" he thought, "Bathing suit, beach towel, sandals, t-shirts—a whole pack, and underpants. How many? Shorts, long pants, sweaters (thin and heavy), socks and a jacket in case it rains. And, oh yeah, rubber boots!"

"How's it going?" Mom called from the kitchen.

"Fine, thanks!" answered Alex.

What did he need for night time? Pajamas, the blue ones with stars and his squirrel…? Holding his favorite stuffed animal, he thought, "Should I really take Croissant with me?" He loved Croissant more than anything, but Alex was old enough. He was going by himself.

He gave Croissant a big kiss and put him back on the bed. "Toothpaste! and the bag with all the bathroom stuff," he finally said.

"Are you finding everything?" Mom asked.

"No problem, Mom," he answered.

She looked at all his things and asked, "Did you pack a jacket in case it rains?"

"Sure, Mom, it's on the bottom."

"What about a heavy wool sweater? You know it can get quite cool at the beach."

"Yeah, I've got that too," sighed Alex.

"Just take care of yourself, Sweetheart, and don't go in the water by yourself, promise?"

"Okay, okay, I promise," said Alex.

"And don't stay out in the sun too long; it's not good for your skin. Oh, did you pack your sun creme?" No. Alex had forgotten that.

Mama sighed, wondering if everything would be okay.

97

At three o'clock the next day Aunt Lily and Uncle Max arrived with Marty, Tim, Lena and Marie. Sometimes Alex thought it would be great having such a big family, but having Mom all to himself was also pretty nice. Besides, he could visit his cousins as often as he liked. Uncle Max loaded Alex's things in the car.

"You haven't forgotten anything, have you?" asked his mother.

"I don't think so," said Alex.

"Don't forget to write," said his mother, and Alex nodded.

His mother smiled, but her voice was a little shaky.

"So, my little sweetheart, have fun!"

"Big Mom, I'm big," corrected Alex and laughed.

A last kiss and then Alex got in the car. As he turned around, he saw his mother had tears in her eyes. Then Alex remembered—he had forgotten something! Without a word he ran back up to his room and got Croissant.

"Here, Mom," said Alex. "This way you won't be alone while I'm gone." Before his mother could say a word Alex was already back in the car. And while Mom hugged Croissant, he waved out the window.

"See you soon," he said.

"See you soon."

Two weeks will fly by…

Evening 23

Like the many evenings before, the two friends sat peacefully together.
"Did you hear that?" whispered the little angel suddenly. "Sounds like someone's hidden a tweeter-machine."

"I'll look for it for you," laughed the old bear and brushed his big paw through
the grass. "I've got it!" He opened his paw and something green jumped out
and landed on the angel's nose.
"Aaaaaa, that tickles," squeaked the angel. "What is it?"

"It's just a little grasshopper," laughed the bear. "Hey, that reminds me of a story!"

And so he began the twenty-third story.

100

Skating *by Bruno Hächler*

Gina sat on a dandelion leaf, bored. She hadn't seen even one of her friends. Then Max, a fat, brown bug came crawling along with Susie the ladybug through the woods. Penelope, the snail, had crawled under a bush. Gina was about to sigh when she discovered something strange.

A little girl was coming down the path at an unbelievable speed. She had on funny shoes with little rubber wheels. The wheels spun around so fast that Gina got dizzy just looking at them. Grasshoppers are very curious. Gina waited until just the right moment and jumped!

How wonderful! It was… indescribable. She had glued herself to the helmet of the little girl. Gina's feelers fluttered and when she opened her mouth she had the feeling she had swallowed the wind.

Gina had only one thought; she wanted to keep rolling just like the girl. By the big linden tree she jumped back into the meadow. She picked twigs and berries from a branch and got to work. Finally the shoes with wheels were finished and she used an acorn as her helmet. "I look almost exactly like the little girl," she thought proudly.

At that moment Max and Susie came wandering along. They examined Gina's roller-skates carefully and Max said, "I want shoes with wheels too!"
"Snails don't have feet," said Penelope sadly from under her bush. "I couldn't wear them."

The whole afternoon Gina, Max, and Susie skated around and around. Though they were tired, Max said, "I think I skate the best!"
Susie peeped. She thought that wasn't true at all and that Max was nothing but a big show-off. She didn't trust herself to say anything to him, however. Gina had no problem. "If anyone here is the best, it's me," she said. "After all, I was the first.

Now Max was mad. "Not true, not true… Look, I'll bet you can't do this!" 101

he said as he rotated on one leg until he couldn't tell his back from his front and tumbled right into the dirt. Gina and Susie just laughed.

Then Gina had an idea. "A race, let's have a race!" she said. They were already at the starting line when they heard a voice huffing and puffing.

"Wait, I want to race too!" said Penelope.
"You?" they asked. They were surprised.
"Yes, me!"
"You don't have feet; how can you wear roller-skates?"
"I don't need shoes with wheels, I have something better," Penelope as she showed them a little board with four wheels. "What is that?"
"A board with skates, of course!"

The race had begun. But it was a sad race indeed. Susie got so excited she kept flapping her wings and flew away. Max rolled a bit, then tripped and fell over on his back. Gina kept making big grasshopper jumps and got tangled up with her own feet. And Penelope? The snail stretched and arched on her board—the same motion she used on the ground—but no matter how hard she tried, the board didn't move.

For a while it was quiet. Then suddenly Gina started laughing and then Max and finally Susie and Penelope too! Suddenly no one wanted to be the best or the quickest. They were all friends, and so with Penelope in the middle, they all skated away, together.

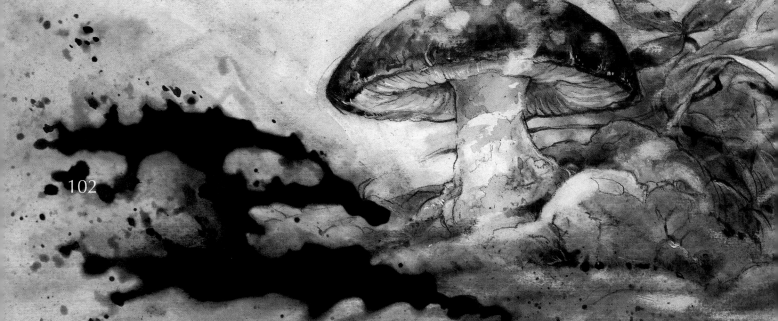

The next evening the bear helped the little angel with his landing practice.

"A little faster," he would say, or "Slower," "Stick your feet out, terrific!"

"Because you're such a good coach," said the angel.

"No, but thanks," said the bear. "Actually, I'm a bit jealous. I would love to look at the world from above and…"

"And what?" asked the angel. He was curious.

"…And bite a sliver from the honey-colored moon."

"I can't take you with me. I'm sorry, but I all I can do is tell you a special story."

And that's how story twenty-four started.

104

A Walk in the Sky *by Brigitte Weninger*

Sometimes Grandpa would take Tim on a walk in the sky—that's what Grandpa called it. Tim would bend forward and Grandpa would pick him up around the ankles and, whoosh, he was up! He could hop on pillows of clouds and swim through the blue sky. Over his head was a colorful meadow where the old nut tree had a lantern hanging in it. It was so pretty that Tim always got a little dizzy.

One day Grandpa said, "I can't lift you anymore; you're too big."
They looked in the mirror.
"It's true" Tim said. "Wow! Soon I'll be as tall as you."

"Be happy," smiled Grandpa. But Tim didn't have much time to feel happy. He had to learn to read and write, to tie his shoes, and to do addition! That wasn't any fun at all.
"Learning something new isn't always easy," said Grandpa, "But when you've learned it, you're happy."

And then came the baby!
His new sister Rose was like a baby pig, and when she squeaked everyone came running and looked surprised. "Oh, isn't that sweet!" they'd say.

Tim thought it was dumb. One time Grandpa lifted the baby up and put her in Tim's arms. His baby sister grinned at him and squeaked. "Now she really looks like a little pig," he thought as he grinned back at her.
He suddenly realized how easily Grandpa had lifted her up and so high. Soon he would take her by the ankles and… Tim started to cry. Grandpa wiped away Tim's tears with his blue and white handkerchief and said, "Now, tell me all about it."

"Grandpa," snitted Tim. "Promise me that you won't ever take the baby on a walk in the sky. I don't want you to, understand?"
Grandpa nodded, he understood.

105

"I promise," he said. "Besides it won't be long before YOU can take your little sister hopping over clouds. I won't be here then."

"Where will you be?" asked Tim.

"Well, I'll be someplace else," answered Grandpa. "I'll be where everything begins and everything ends. But when I go I'll leave you my handkerchief with a knot tied in the corner. That way, we won't forget each other, okay?"

"Okay," said Tim, and then they played cards sitting on the baby blanket.

With the years, Grandpa seemed to grow smaller than Tim. Tim went shopping for him, read him the newspaper and sometimes tied his shoelaces.

"Good thing I learned everything," said Tim.

"Yes, you certainly have grown!" said Grandpa, smiling as he tied a knot in the corner of his blue and white handkerchief.

Not long after that Grandpa passed away. Tim's little sister often looked for him and cried. Tim missed him too, but at least he knew where his grandfather had gone. Tim wiped away her tears with the blue and white handkerchief and said, "Grandpa is now where you were, before you came to us. Everything is fine there." His little sister listened, but she didn't really understand; she was too young.

"Do you want to play a special game?" he asked. "It's called A Walk in Sky." His little sister nodded. He grabbed her ankles and, whoosh, she was up!

"Pretty," she squeaked, "all blue and white!"

She was happy and laughed.

It made Tim laugh too.

Evening 25

On the next evening, it rained.

"What yucky weather," complained the little angel.

"Do angels get wet when it rains?" asked the bear.

"No," the angel had to admit, "but flying in good weather is hard enough, and when the clouds are heavy and you can't even see the angel in front of you, then it's really difficult."

"I see," said the bear and then said, "Come over here by me. My fur is so thick no rain comes through."

"Why, thanks," beamed the little angel and snuggled in close.

"How about a secret story?" asked the angel. "I've got one!" said the bear and began the twenty-fifth story.

The Chicken has a Secret

by Karl Rühmann

The chicken lived on a farm with many other animals, but she often felt lonely. No matter how well she clucked or how cleverly she caught worms, no one seemed to notice. Even though the way she scratched for seeds was very elegant indeed, no one cared, Her neighbor had it better. Every time that pig played in the mud people would shout, "Look at the funny little pig!"

When the cat purred, you'd hear, "What, a sweet little cat!"
And the dog had to only to wag his tail once or catch a silly stick and everyone would say, "What a clever little dog!"

They all seemed to overlook the chicken. But that wasn't even the worst thing. Far worse was that no one, not even the other animals, would have anything to do with the chicken. The little pig, the cat, the bunny and the dog all played with one another, laughed and gossiped. But when the chicken came by, the dog would growl and say, "Look out, here comes the chicken," and they would stop playing.

"They have a secret," thought the chicken. "I wish I had one, but where can I find a real secret?"
She shook her head sadly. "If I could find a secret treasure or discover a secret passageway or if I could become a secret agent..." she thought. "Cluccck, the magpie is a clever bird and has a nest full of secrets. Perhaps she'll give me one?" So the chicken started out right away and she was lucky; she found the magpie at home.

"Oh, Magpie, nobody wants to play with me," said the chicken, looking up the tree. "They're mean to me and they keep secrets. I don't have one; can you give me one?"
The magpie stuck her head out of her nest and cawed, "And what do I get forit?"
"All my pocket-corn: four kernels," said the chicken. "Five," said the magpie.
The chicken pressed her beak together firmly and said, "Oh, all right," and   109

took out her coin-purse.

Then the magpie flew down, carrying the most curious thing. It looked like two yogurt containers connected with a string.

"What is it?" asked the chicken.

"That's the secret," said the magpie. "Just clap them over your ears, wait and see what happens."

The chicken thanked the magpie politely, and after a little while she put on "the secret" and listened. At first she heard the wind and then something else…

"Wow! This is great," she said. "The wind is talking to me, to me alone."

110 The chicken was so busy with her secret she didn't notice the others.

Suddenly there they were! "What's that?" asked the little pig.
"I can't tell you," whispered the chicken. "It's a secret!"

"Can I try too?" asked the dog. The chicken hesitated, but then said, "Well,
   okay!" and handed over the secret. One after another tried the secret.
The pig sighed, "How beautifully the wind is oinking in my ears."
The chicken nodded proudly. "Remember, you can't tell a soul," she said,
"it's a secret!"
All four agreed, "It's a deal!"
From then on they all played together and shared the chicken's secret.
But remember, "Don't tell, it's a secret."   111

When the little angel landed the next evening, the old bear was lying under a nut tree, snoring.

"Hey, bear," the angel said in a sing-songy voice. The bear kept sleeping. The angel puckered up and made a nasty sound. The bear woke up with a start. "What was that?" he asked.

"You said you woke up with the littlest flea-peep," said the angel, laughing. "I just wanted to see if that was true."

"Was I snoring," the bear said, a bit embarrassed. "Only a little," said the angel politely, "but I know a story about someone who REALLY snored!" So the little angel began the twenty-sixth story.

112

Snorey *by Géraldine Elschner*

Snorey was not the quickest. He ate slowly, ran slowly, and understood things, well...slowly. He was very fast at falling asleep, however, and he was a great snorer.

One day he really perked up, for a beautiful girl moved into the house next door. She was a dream! Everyone liked her, particularly Snorey. From that day on he could think of nothing else. Instead of looking sleepy all the time he always had a dreamy look about him. Of course this looks the same from the outside, but from inside it is very different.
"When I grow up, I'm going to marry her and take her away on a unicorn," he said. "Together we will see the world!"

Every evening he fell asleep with this thought. He didn't fall asleep as quickly as he used to, but what beautiful dreams he had!
Then one morning...

"You snore like a bear," a friend told him after sleeping over with Snorey. That hurt. Could it be true that Snorey... snored? How awful, how terrible! How could he ever marry the beautiful girl next door?

So Snorey went in search of an anti-snoring product. He read the newspaper and listened to every advertisement. One day there were two old ladies standing in front of the drugstore. "When we first got married, my husband snored something awful. He sounded like a saw," said Mrs. Rose. "It didn't last long however, because my grandmother gave me a tip..."
Snorey moved a little closer so he could hear better.
"You need a cork and also..."

At that very moment a red convertible raced by and VROOOM!!! disappeared around the corner, and with it his solution to snoring. The two old ladies walked away, laughing.

One needed a cork—that much he had heard. So that night he went to bed   113 with a cork. What was he supposed to do with it, though? Probably stick it in something—after all, that's what corks are for, but where? In his ears? In his nose?

No, it was much too big and he was sure it wouldn't help if he stuck it anywhere else. So he tried his mouth. He made a kind of pacifier and had his first sleepless night, ever. The thing tasted awful! On the second night he tried it in his left ear and on the third night in his right ear. He didn't get a wink of sleep!

Poor Snorey was so tired that on the fourth day he gathered up all his courage and rang Mrs. Rose's door bell.
"Hello," he said. "Can you help me? I have a question." He had to whisper his problem. Until now no one knew about the beautiful girl, and he turned red just whispering.

Mrs. Rose smiled and said, "Oh, that's easy! Just take the cork and..." The rest she also whispered. Old ladies understand about secrets.
"Oh, I understand," said Snorey. "Thank you so much, Mrs. Rose. He ran home laughing and that night he attached the cork tightly.

Where? "One snores only when they sleep on their back," Mrs. Rose had explained, "so you must attach the cork tightly. As soon as you try to roll over on your back, it will hurt, and you will automatically roll over and stop snoring."

Did it work? After three sleepless nights Snorey slept so deeply that he could have had ten cola cans on his back and he would have felt nothing.
One thing is for sure: Snorey later married that beautiful girl next door, and since then the two have traveled the world.
So... give it a try!

Evening 27

On the next evening the little angel and the bear sat quietly looking at the moon. Finally the old bear cleared his throat and said, "Will the big honey-moon be finished tomorrow or can it get even bigger?"

"No, tomorrow is the full moon," said the angel. "It doesn't get any rounder than that!"

"Too bad," sighed the old bear and was quiet.

"Enough of looking sadly at the moon," said the angel. "Tell me something funny instead, with a kangaroo maybe."

"What, a story about a kangaroo? Well, let me think."

The old bear told the twenty-seventh story.

116

The Warmest Bed in the World

by Géraldine Elschner

Mama Rumba danced around happily. Soon her first baby would be born!
She needed to be ready, so she gathered hay and straw and stuck everything
in her pouch. But when she got home, it was empty.
"Oh no, I must have a hole in my pouch," she sighed. "I'll have to mend it."
On the next day Mama Rumba got up and got her home all ready. Everything
had to be just so. That evening she sat down tired and put her cold hands in
her warm pouch, but…

"Oh no, the hole! Tomorrow I will get needle and thread, tomorrow, tomorrow…"
But on the next morning the baby came sooner than expected and she was
so happy as it crawled in her warm pouch. Then came another baby and then
another—she had triplets! This was quite unusual in the kangaroo world.
Mama Rumba was three times happier, and she stayed at home three times
longer with her children.
One day she said, "Come here, my sweet things. You're big enough, it's time
for our first trip." Hop, hop, hop, they all were on their way.
"Hello, look who I've brought with me," she said to her relatives. But when
she wanted to show them the triplets… Her pouch was empty.

"Help!" cried Mama Rumba. "The hole, that stupid awful hole! Where are my
children?"
Like lightning she hopped all the way back. Her first baby was sleeping peacefully in the grass. A hedgehog had made a bed of moss for the little one.
"Oh, thank you," said Mama Rumba. "He fell out of my pouch, there's a hole…"
"Well, that should be sewed up right away," said the hedgehog. "Here, take
one of my needles—and do it soon."
"Yes, thank you and I promise." She put the baby in her pouch held him tightly
with one paw and hopped away quickly.

Her second baby was sleeping under a tree. A bird was singing the baby a lullaby. 117

"Thank you," said Mama Rumba. "It's just a little hole and I have a needle to sew it up!"

"A hole?" asked the bird. "Give me that needle, I'll put a hole in it for the thread, but you must hurry."

"Yes, yes, I will, I promise," said Mama Rumba and put her second baby in her pouch. She held them snuggly with her paws and hopped away.

Her third baby was sleeping under a berry shrub. A spider had woven a little blanket for it.

"Thank you," said Mama Rumba, "There was an itty bitty hole in my pouch and…"

"How dreadful," scolded the spider. "Here is some thread, do it right now!"

"Yes, yes, yes, I promise," said Mama Rumba. She laid her third baby with the other two, held them snuggly and hopped home. This time she would not put it off until morning. She took the sharp needle and began to thread it.

"Wait, stop, that will hurt!" said a sheep that was passing by.

"I know," said the kangaroo, "but I have a hole in my pouch that must be mended!"

"Wait," said the sheep. "What if you fill the hole with wool?"

"With wool?"

"Sure, I have plenty. Just stuff it tightly in the hole and your babies will have an even softer bed."

And that is exactly what Mama Rumba did. And she did it right away!

She was so happy that she danced with the sheep while her children slept in the warmest bed in the world.

Evening 28

The last evening was approaching. The old bear had been sitting in the meadow since the afternoon, waiting for the little angel. This time the angel didn't come flying down like a canon ball, or a hippo, or a sack of potatoes. No, he floated down without a sound, flew elegantly around the plum tree and landed as gently as a butterfly in the meadow.

"Wonderful," said the old bear and applauded.

"That was definitely A-number-1-heavenly, don't you think?" asked the angel, grinning. "They'll be so darned surprised! Oops!" he exlaimed, covering his mouth. "How did that sneak out?"

Your Angel-eze still needs some work." said the bear, laughing. "Perhaps you shouldn't talk too much during your test. I like you just the way you are!"

The little angel hugged his big friend and whispered in his furry ear, "I'm a little sad that I have to leave today."

"Me too," said the bear. "But saying goodbye is a part of life, and we will meet again. Besides, I have my little round comfort box and our stories."

"I'll come and visit you," promised the angel. "But I can hardly wait to be a Guardian Angel."

"And that's the way it should be," said the bear. "Whose turn is it tonight to tell the story?"

120

One Sheep, Two Sheep, Three Sheep... *by Hubert Flattinger*

The old bear counted sheep, because he couldn't sleep. But since he could only count up to 21, he was starting his fourth time through.
"One sheep, two sheep, three sheep..."
The old bear had just counted the fourteenth sheep and then... Nothing happened!
"Hey, wait a minute," said the bear, "Where is sheep number fifteen and sixteen? And hey, where are all the rest of the sheep? Sheep seventeen, eighteen, nineteen and twenty, where are you?"
But no one answered.

The bear was starting to get worried. "What if something has happened to them?" he wondered. "What if they are lost in the dark and don't know where to go? Oh, the poor sheep! I have to help them." And though he was starting to get sleepy, he got out from under his big feather bed and started searching for the lost sheep.

There were a thousand twinkling stars in the sky.
"Oh, Big Bear that twinkles in the sky, can you see my sheep anywhere?"
But the Big Bear was still.
The old bear looked and looked. He even looked in the dog house but there was only Bruno, dreaming of a bone and snoring.

"If I just wasn't so tired," said the old bear. He could hardly keep his eyes open. He yawned and wished he could go back to bed. But first he had to find the sheep.

He roamed late into the night and found this and that, but not his sheep. He was so sleepy, he decided to turn around and go home.
Just as the old bear was starting to snuggle under the covers, he heard a familiar... "Baaa, Baa!" Well, if that wasn't sheep number fifteen! 121

He looked under his bed and sure enough, there was number fifteen
and all the rest of the missing sheep.

"Oh, my goodness," he said, "You are certainly a group!
Were you here the whole time?"
Number fifteen answered in a sleepy voice,

"Yes, but don't be angry with us, please.
After you had counted us so often,
we were so tired that we put ourselves to sleep."
The sweet old bear didn't say a word,
for he had finally...fallen asleep!

The old bear and the little angel sat looking up at the full moon. It was round and yellow again, just like a honeycomb that was hanging in the sky. The little angel sighed deeply, "So, that was it."

"Yes, for now we're finished," said the old bear, smiling. "Actually, I could start tomorrow evening telling stories again until the next big honey colored moon."

"But who will be listening while I'm away?" asked the little angel, a bit worried.

"Oh, I guess I can find somebody," winked the old bear. "Everyone likes to hear a good story. You told me yourself that no one is really alone. If no one else comes I can always tell my guardian angel."

"That's true," said the little angel, nodding. Then he hugged the old bear around the neck and whispered in his furry ear, "Now I'll tell you the special word, the one you should always remember. It is… GROW!

…Do you understand what it is supposed to mean?"

"Sure," said the bear. "When you're little you should grow on the outside, and when you're big you must grow on the inside. That way one always feels alive and grows a little wiser every day."

"Exactly," said the little angel and hugged his friend tightly.
"I'll be thinking of some new stories for our next visit!"
said the old bear, feeling a little sad. "And now, off with
you, little friend...all the best!"

"Bye, bye," said the little angel, waving. Then he flew gently
away toward the big, round, honey-colored moon.
And before they lost sight of each other they called out
the special word,

"......!"